# DORA
## SU

E
Illustr

A GOLDEN BOOK

D1017545

0272056

¡*Hola!* I'm Dora, and this is my best friend, Boots. Today is a day that only comes once a year—my birthday!

Look! Silly Mail Bird has a message for me. Let's read it together.

Dear Dora,
¡Feliz cumpleaños! Happy birthday!
Get ready for your Birthday Scavenger Hunt! We have a present for you, but you'll have to look for three clues to find it. We'll all celebrate together when you find the last clue.
Love,
Mami and Papi

A scavenger hunt! *¡Fantástico!* Will you help me look for clues? Great!

I wonder where we should start looking. Who do we ask for help when we don't know which way to go? *¡Sí!* Map!

Map says that the first clue is in the tallest tree in the Nutty Forest. The second clue is at Troll Bridge. And the third clue is on top of Rainbow Rock. *¡Vámonos!* Let's go!

Hey! There's Tico! Tico says he'll give us a ride to the Nutty Forest. *¡Gracias, amigo!* Thanks!

We made it to the Nutty Forest! Now, which tree is the tallest?

Yeah, the tree in the middle is the tallest! *¡Excelente!*

Boots climbed up
the tallest tree to look
for the first clue. Great
climbing, Boots!

There's a box hanging from a branch. Help Boots climb to the branch. *¡Sube, sube!* Climb, climb!

There's a ball of yarn inside the box! The yarn is my first clue. Let's look for the next one.

We need to go to Troll Bridge for the second clue. But first we have to get through the Purple Gate. Will you check Backpack for something that will open the lock? Say "Backpack!"

"Do you see anything that will open the lock?

Yeah, that's right, the purple key! *¡Muy bien!*"

We're at Troll Bridge! The Grumpy Old Troll says we have to solve his riddle to get the box. Will you help?

"This dessert is sweet
And a birthday treat to eat.
But first it needs to bake.
It's a birthday . . ."

Hmm. What's a sweet dessert you
bake and eat on a birthday? *¡Sí!* A CAKE!

Uh-oh! Swiper wants to swipe the box that's holding my second birthday clue!

He says he won't swipe my box because it's my birthday. *¡Gracias, Swiper!*

Now let's see what's inside the box. It's a little bowl! The first clue was a ball of yarn, and the second clue is a bowl. I wonder what my present is. Let's go find the last clue at Rainbow Rock!

*¡Mira!* Look! There are stars everywhere!
Artista, the Skywriting Explorer Star, wrote
a birthday message for me in the sky!

How many stars do you see? *Uno, dos, tres, cuatro, cinco, seis, siete, ocho, nueve, diez.* Ten stars! We need to reach up and catch the stars. Reach high in the air! Super catching!

We're at Rainbow Rock! To get to the top, we need to climb the colored rocks. Do you see them?

Call out the color of each rock to show us which way to go! Red! Orange! Yellow! Green! Blue! Purple! *¡Fantástico!*

We made it to the top! Do you see a box
hidden anywhere? There's a box in that bush.
Let's open it to find the last clue!

The third clue is a carton of milk! What are all the clues, again? Yarn, a bowl, and milk. What do you think Mami and Papi got me? I have an idea. . . . I really hope I'm right! Let's find out at my party!

Yay! All my friends and family are at my birthday party. Mmm, Papi made a chocolate cake! I'm making a wish before I blow out my candles. What will you wish for on your birthday?

*¡Mira!* I was right! Mami and Papi gave me a kitten—just like I thought the clues were telling me! I'm going to name him Gatito. He loves playing with the yarn and drinking milk from his bowl!

Thanks for helping me find the birthday clues and for coming to my party! *¡Gracias!*